I Like You

by Sandol Stoddard Warburg

illustrated by Jacqueline Chwast

1965   Houghton Mifflin Company Boston

Twelfth Printing w

to Jean
and Frank
and Marian
and Paul
and Matthew
and Joy
and Austin
and people
like that

I like you

And I know why

I like you because

You are a good person

To like

I like you because

When I tell you something special
You know it's special
And you remember it
A long long time

You say
Remember when you told me
Something special

And both of us remember

When I think something is important
You think it's important too

We have good ideas

8

When I say something funny

You laugh

I think I'm funny and
You think I'm funny too

Hah-hah

9

I like you because
You know where I'm ticklish
And you don't tickle me there
    except
    Just a little tiny bit
    sometimes

stop
stop stop
help
help

But if you do then I know where to tickle you too

HELP

You know how to be silly
That's why I like you

Boy are you ever silly

I never met anybody sillier than me
    till I met you

I like you because
You know when it's time to stop being silly

Maybe day after tomorrow
Maybe never

Oops too late
it's quarter past silly

13

We fool around the same way all the time

Sometimes we don't say a word
We snurkle under fences
We spy secret places

14

If I am a goofus on the roofus
Hollering my head off
You are one too

If I pretend I am drowning
You pretend you are saving me

If I am getting ready to pop a paper bag
Then you are getting ready to jump

HOORAY

That's because
You really like me

You really like me
Don't you

And I really like you back
And you like me back
And I like you back

And that's the way we keep on going
Every day

If you go away
    then I go away too
Or if I stay home
You send me a postcard

You don't just say
Well see you around
Some time
Bye

I like you a lot
    because of that
If I go away
I send you a postcard too

And I like you because
If we go away together
And if we are in Grand Central Station
And if I get lost
Then you are the one that is yelling for me

Hey where are you

23

And I like you because
When I am feeling sad
You don't always cheer me up right away

Sometimes it is better to be sad
You can't stand the others being so googly and gaggly
    every single minute
You want to think about things

It takes time

I like you because if I am mad at you
Then you are mad at me too

It's awful when the other person isn't

Phooey

They are so nice and hoo-hoo you could just about
   punch them in the nose

I like you because if I think I am going to
   throw up then you are really sorry

Or synonyms

You don't just pretend you are busy looking at
   the birdies and all that

You say maybe it was something you ate

You say the same thing happened to me one time

And the same thing did

If you find two four-leaf clovers
You give me one

If I find four
I give you two

If we only find three
We keep on looking

Sometimes we have good luck
And sometimes we don't

If I break my arm and
If you break your arm too
Then it is fun to have a broken arm

I tell you about mine
You tell me about yours

We are both sorry

We write our names and draw pictures

We show everybody and they wish they had a broken arm too

I like you because
I don't know why but
Everything that happens
Is nicer with you

I can't remember when I didn't like you

It must have been lonesome then

I like you because because because

I forget why I like you

But I do

So many reasons

On the Fourth of July I like you because
It's the Fourth of July

On the Fifth of July
I like you too

If you and I had some drums
And some horns and some horses

If we had some hats and some
Flags and some fire-engines

We could be a HOLIDAY   We could be a CELEBRATION

We could be a WHOLE PARADE   See what I mean?

Even if it was the
nine-hundred-and-ninety-
ninth of July

Even if it was August

Even if it was way down at the bottom of November
Even if it was no place particular in January

I would go on choosing you
And you would go on choosing me
Over and over again

That's how it would happen every time
I don't know why

I guess I don't know why I like you really
Why do I like you

I guess I just like you

I guess I just like you

Because I like you